Created by
Jim Jinkins

BRAND SPANKING NEW!

DouG™

CHRONICLES

Lost in Space

Tim Grundmann

JUMBO
PICTURES INC.

DISNEY
PRESS

New York

SPECIAL EDITION

Illustrated by Matthew C. Peters, Tim Chi Ly,
Cheng-li Chan, and Tony Curanaj

The artwork for this book is prepared using watercolor.
The test for this book is set in 18-point New Century Schoolbook.

Library of Congress Catalog Card Number: 97-80216
ISBN: 0-7868-4278-4

Created by
Jim Jinkins

Lost in Space

CHAPTER 1

"Ta-daahh! What do you think, Doug?"

"Skeeter, that's an awesome solar system costume!" said Doug Funnie. "But it makes mine look wimpy."

"No way, man." Skeeter said.

"Yours is portable. Like, if you're at the video store and you forget where Neptune is, you can look up and check."

Doug smiled. Skeeter Valentine was the best friend a guy could have. After they changed out of their costumes Doug said, "Come on, Skeet, my dad's setting up his telescope so we can check out the stars."

"I'm right with you, man," honked Skeeter.

The boys raced out the back-door.

"Hey, boys," Doug's dad called, "ready to see the heavens like

you've never seen them before?"

He let Skeeter look first. Skeeter shouted, "Whoa! That star's really twinkling!"

But then he said, "Oh, no, it's only a lightning bug."

Doug laughed. But when he looked through the telescope, he saw that it wasn't a bug. "Hey, wait a minute," Doug cried, "that's not a lightning bug, it looks like . . . a comet!"

"Hmm, that's odd," Mr. Funnie said. "No comets have been reported."

But he looked for himself, and turned to the boys and beamed. "Well, it looks like maybe you two just discovered a new comet and whoever discovers a new comet gets to name it!"

Doug said, "Wow! The Funnie-Valentine Comet!"

But at the same time, Skeeter shouted, "Wow! The Valentine-Funnie Comet!"

Doug looked at Skeeter in surprise. "Uh, sure, your name can go first, Skeet. I don't mind."

"Okay, man," Skeeter said, "it seems only fair since I saw it first."

"Wait a minute," Doug said. "You thought it was just a lightning bug."

Doug's dad was amazed to see the two pals arguing. Doug's sister Judy came and Doug's mom followed her with baby Dirtbike.

"Funnie-Valentine!"

"Valentine-Funnie!"

"Can you believe this?" Judy asked her mother. "They're acting like babies."

Baby Dirtbike nodded her head.

CHAPTER 2

News of Doug and Skeeter's
discovery spread all over
Bluffington. At Swirly's the next
day the friends still weren't
speaking to each other.

"Doug, does it matter whose
name is first?" asked Patti

Mayonnaise. "I think you should apologize to Skeeter."

"Me, apologize to Skeeter?" Doug asked. "No way!"

Just then, Mr. Swirly made an announcement over the loud-speaker:

"Attention ice cream lovers! Today I'm introducing a brand-new Swirly's dessert sensation! Mt. Swirly—the tallest ice cream mountain peak in the world! Who wants to scale the first one?"

Everyone cried "Me!" but two people shouted it the loudest—Doug and Skeeter. They both grabbed the towering dessert at

the same time, sending the tippy-
top scoop of ice cream flying like
a comet out of control.

Splat! It hit Patti Mayonnaise
right on top of her head!

Doug watched in horror as the

ice cream dripped
down her face. He
had never seen
Patti that angry.

Then Skeeter
said, "Way to go,
Doug."

"Me?" Doug
shouted. "What
about you!"

Patti was furious.
"This wouldn't have happened if
you two weren't acting like
babies," she shouted. She stormed
out the door.

Doug walked home alone. He
felt awful about what had happened

to Patti, and it was Skeeter's fault! When he got to his bedroom he slammed the door and shouted, "Skeeter Valentine is a big giant loser!"

Porkchop jumped a foot off the floor.

"Sorry, pal," Doug said, giving his dog a reassuring pat. Doug noticed some of his Quailman doodles lying on the floor. "Hey, Porkchop, I wonder what Quailman would do if he got worked up about something like this?"

Porkchop shrugged, but Doug kept wondering. He needed to

11

calm down. So he lay next to
Porkchop and started doodling. It
made him smile just to think
about Quailman.

CHAPTER 3

THE ADVENTURES OF QUAILMAN!

As our story begins, Quailman and Silver Skeeter are at Cape Bluffington to launch the first kid into outer space–Patti Mayonnaise! But something was wrong. The world's two greatest superheroes were not speaking to each other.

"He called me 'Belt-head,'" said Quailman.

"And he called me 'Liquid-metal-brain,'" said Silver Skeeter, the world's only superhero made of liquid titanium.

The two superheroes stood with their arms folded defiantly. Astronaut Patti banged on the window of the rocket and shouted, "Let's get this show on the road!"

"Somebody's got to launch this thing," said Mayor Tippy, and she pushed the rocket launch button.

WHOOSH!

It was a perfect blastoff. But
Quailman's trusty companion,
Quaildog, sensed that something
was not quite right. His keen,
quaillike eyesight spotted something alarming in the skies.

"What's that, Quaildog?" Quailman looked up as Quaildog pointed to the skies. "Oh, no! The rocket carrying Miss Mayonnaise is in danger of being struck by a comet! No time to lose. Fly awaaaay!"

"Hi-ho, Silver-power!" cried Silver Skeeter, and our heroes were off. But would they make it in time?

They flew swift and sure, but they were too late. The comet crashed into the side of the rocket and sent the rocket hurtling into uncharted territory.

"Hang on!" cried Quailman.

CHAPTER 4

"Must. . . summon. . . my. . .
quail powers," grunted Quailman.
"Must. . . stop. . . this. . . thing . . ."

But the rocket was traveling at
such a tremendous speed that even
the powers of Quailman and Silver

Skeeter combined could not stop it.

"I'm getting space-sick," shouted Silver Skeeter.

The rocket carried them into unknown galaxies. After millions

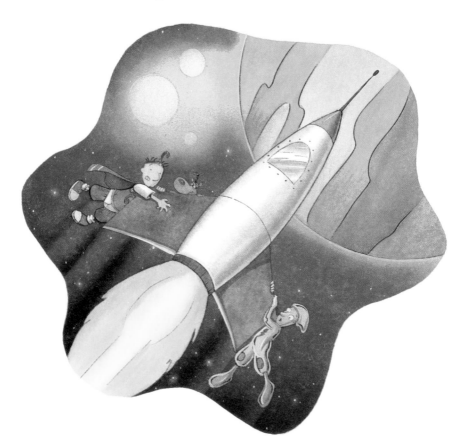

of miles, they finally approached
a strange planet with three suns.

"We're going to crash!" yelled
Quailman.

Just when it seemed they were
doomed, Silver Skeeter stretched
himself into a parachute and
gently lowered the rocket.

The shuttle door opened and
Patti got out. "Good work, Silver
Skeeter," she said.

"For what?" asked Quailman.
"Just for saving our lives? Big
deal."

"I think somebody's jealous,"
Silver Skeeter said.

Patti told them the rocket was

badly damaged and they would have to repair it. "Now," she said, "where are we?"

Quailman looked around the strange landscape. "We're, uh . . ."

"Yeah, we're, uh. . . ," said Silver Skeeter.

"I don't know," they finally admitted.

"Great," Patti said. "We're lost in space."

Then they saw something that took their breath away. Babies and toddlers. Some holding rattles, some with pacifiers in their mouths. All coming toward the strange alien visitors.

"It's the Planet of the Babies!"
shouted Quailman.

"Takes a real genius to figure
that out," said a baby.

Our heroes stared at the baby
in surprise. Was it their
imaginations, or did this baby
look familiar?

"Nice outfits," the wise-guy baby said. "Where'd you come from, Planet Underwear?"

CHAPTER 5

"For your information,"
Quailman said stiffly, "we happen
to be highly decorated, world-
famous superheroes!"

"Oh, yeah?" said the wise-guy
baby.

Patti whispered slyly, "I think

23

these toddlers need a demonstra-
tion of your super-powers."

"Hmm," said Quailman.
"Perhaps it is justified in this
case."

Both superheroes took a flying
leap—and fell flat on their faces.

"Huh?" said Quailman.

"We've lost our super-powers!"
shouted Silver Skeeter.

The wise-guy baby rolled
on the ground laughing.
"Some superheroes!
Super-zeroes is
more like it!
Goo-goo!"

"I bet this

planet has some sort of magnetic field that has affected your super-abilities," Patti said.

Even Quaildog's quail-tail was limp and useless. He wimpered pitifully.

"This is embarrassing," Quailman said. "Without our super-powers, we just look like a couple of, um–"

"Nitwits?" a baby said.

"Losers?" said the wise-guy baby.

"We're not losers," Quailman said angrily.

Then Patti spotted a dome-shaped building in the distance.

"That looks like an observatory,"
she said. "I bet someone there can
help us."

CHAPTER 6

The observatory was made out
of alphabet blocks. Our heroes
walked inside and found two baby
astronomers standing by the
telescope.

"Excuse me, —er, gentlebabies,"
said Quailman, "but we appear to

27

be lost in space. Could you–"

But the two babies were in the middle of an argument.

"I saw it first," one of them said.

"No, me!" cried the other. "Waaaah!"

Our heroes waited patiently. It appeared that the two baby astronomers had just discovered a new comet. Now they were arguing over what to name it.

Quailman shook his head in disgust. "Tsk, tsk! Imagine, fighting over something as ridiculous as that."

"Unbelievable," Silver Skeeter said.

What was unbelievable, Patti
thought, was that the two
arguing tots looked just like Doug
and Skeeter! She stepped
between them and looked through
the telescope.

What she saw made her gasp.
"That comet is coming straight
toward this planet!"

Quailman looked for himself.
"Right you are, Miss Mayonnaise,"
he said grimly. "And it appears to
be the same comet that struck
your rocket. We must have

altered its orbit."

They looked at each other in horror. Soon the Planet of the Babies would be destroyed–with them on it! What could they do?

The two baby astronomers were still arguing.

Our heroes went outside to sit down and think.

"We're responsible, you know," Patti sighed. "If we hadn't hit that comet, it wouldn't be coming this way."

"It's Silver Skeeter's fault," Quailman said. "He's the one who–"

"My fault?" shouted Silver Skeeter. "It's his fault!"

"No, it was his end of the rocket that hit the comet–"

"But if he were faster–"

Patti had enough. She shouted, "Would you two stop it!"

And even Quaildog barked in agreement.

The superheroes stopped.

"That comet is going to smash this planet to smithereens," Patti said, "and you two are arguing like babies. Why can't you get along?"

CHAPTER 7

"I could give you a list," said Quailman.

Patti got out paper and pens and said, "Here, write down the top five reasons you don't like each other. You'll see how silly you're being."

The superheroes began writing.

After a minute they were finished.
Patti read Quailman's list first.

TOP 5 REASONS WHY I DON'T LIKE
SILVER SKEETER
1. Can you say "obnoxious"?
2. He borrowed my quail-cape without asking and waxed his skateboard with it.
3. You just can't trust anyone who's liquid.
4. He has loud parties next door to my Thicket of Solitude.
5. His "Silver Skeeter Honk" is *very* much like my "Quail Call."

Then Patti read Silver
Skeeter's list:

**TOP 5 REASONS WHY I DON'T LIKE
QUAILMAN**

1. What's with that belt on his head? Does
   it hold his brain up or what?
2. Can you say irritating?
3. Those plastic quails in his front yard
   are an eyesore.
4. Anyone who wears underwear over his
   pants has a few screws loose.
5. Many, many other reasons I can't think
   of right now.

"Hopeless," Patti sighed. "If we're
going to get rid of that comet,
we've got to work as a team."

"We could build a super-
catapult," Quailman said, "and

launch something really big to knock the comet out of its orbit."

"That's not a bad idea," said Patti, "but what's big enough to do that?"

Quaildog had an idea. He stood on his hind legs with his ears arched to a point. He looked just like a rocket.

"Hey, look," Quailman said. "I think Quaildog is trying to tell us something."

Quaildog crouched down, then shot up into the air.

Patti's eyes lit up. "Quaildog, you're a genius! We'll use a catapult to launch the rocket—and knock the comet out of its path!"

The superheroes weren't sure. "But then we'll lose the rocket," Silver Skeeter said. "We still have to repair it, remember?"

"We'll be in the rocket," Patti said. "And once we're off this planet, you and Quailman

will have your super-powers back and you can guide it back to Earth. Come on, let's round up the babies. We'll need their help."

CHAPTER 8

But the babies said it was their nap time.

"If we don't take our naps," one of them said, "we get cwanky."

"You wouldn't like us cwanky," said another baby.

"I don't care if you're cwanky or

not," said Quailman. "You've got to help us launch the wocket! Let's get to work."

"Excuse me?" the wise-guy baby said. "We don't take orders from you."

"Who do you take orders from?" said Quailman.

"Me," said a baby.

"No!" said yet another baby. "It's my turn to be in charge."

It was the two baby astronomers.

"No!" said the first one. "You were in charge when we battled the Giant Eyeballs, wemember?"

Quailman exploded. "Now, stop

that! You think it's more important to be in charge than to save your planet? You're acting just like . . ."

He suddenly stopped and realized what he was saying. He turned to Silver Skeeter and said, "You know what? We've been acting like babies."

"You're right," Silver Skeeter said. "I'm sorry I called you 'Belthead.' And I promise not to have any more loud parties next door to your Thicket of Solitude."

Patti grinned at Quaildog.

"I'm sorry I called you 'Liquidmetal-brain,'" said Quailman. "And I promise to get rid of those tacky plastic quails in my front yard. Are we pals again?"

"Super-pals!" said Silver Skeeter, and they shook on it.

The two battling babies were silent. "Let's work together," one of them said and *they* shook on it.

CHAPTER 9

By daybreak everything was ready and our heroes climbed inside the rocket. An army of babies hoisted it with the pulley, setting it onto the catapult.

"Operation Comet-Smash ready for action," said Quailman.

"You mean Operation Baby-Power," said Silver Skeeter.

"Operation Comet-Smash."

"Baby-Power!"

They stopped, and burst out laughing.

"Come on, guys," shouted Patti, "the comet's coming!"

As the baby astronomers got ready to release the catapult, our heroes shouted the count-down: "Ten, nine, eight, seven, six, five, four, three, two, one, blastoff!"

Boiiing!

Whooooooosh!!

The rocket flew into space and

Patti expertly steered the rocket
toward the edge of the comet
as they nervously braced
themselves.

Bump!

But they hardly felt a thing.
The nose of the rocket was so well
padded with mattresses and
pillows that it softened the
impact. They knocked the comet
on its side and sent it spinning
away.

"Well done, Astronaut
Mayonnaise!" shouted Quailman.
"Hey, I feel my quail-powers
coming back!"

Silver Skeeter said his powers

were returning, too, and even
Quaildog proudly flexed his
quail-tail.

"Just in time, too," said Patti.
"This rocket's flying out of
control. You guys want to take
over?"

The three superheroes guided the damaged rocket back to planet Earth and Cape Bluffington. The waiting crowd cheered their arrival, and Mayor Tippy asked what they had found in outer space.

"We discovered something called 'give-and-take,'" Quailman told the crowd. "Even if you think you're right, the other person may think he's right, too, and it's sure not worth losing a friendship over."

"I thought we discovered something called 'point of view,'" Silver Skeeter disagreed.

"No, good friend, it was definitely 'give-and-take,'" Quailman assured him.

"No, 'point of view,'" Silver Skeeter insisted.

Quailman and Silver Skeeter looked at each other and burst out laughing.

"Well, I thought we learned how to settle our differences without acting like babies. But I guess some things you have to practice," explained Quailman.

"Yes," agreed his silver buddy. "We've got it now, though, and the world is safe once again."

"Fly awaaaay!"
"Hi-Ho, Silver-power!"

CHAPTER 10

Doug put down his pencil. His Quailman comic book was finished. "You know what, Porkchop?" said Doug. "There are lots more important things in life than getting your own way.

Friendship is way more important!"

But Porkchop pointed at his half-eaten Peanutty Buddy Bar.

"Yeah," Doug laughed. "Peanutty Buddy Bars are important, too."

Doug decided he would tell Skeeter that it could be the Valentine-Funnie comet. "Come on, Porkchop," he said, "Let's straighten this out."

But as they rushed down the stairs to the front door, Skeeter arrived. He was grinning. "Hey, Doug, guess what? I decided your name should go first."

Doug stopped in his tracks. "No, your name should be first," he said.

"No, yours."

"Yours."

"Yours!"

Doug's dad called from the living room. "Hey, boys, come in here. You've got to see this."

Doug and Skeeter went into the living room, where Doug's parents were watching the evening news.

"Two boys from Bluffington have just discovered a new comet . . ."

The TV showed a star map indicating where the comet was spotted. Skeeter shouted, "Hey, that's our comet!"

"But we never reported it," Doug said.

"Sorry, boys," Doug's dad said. "Some other guys beat you to it."

Doug felt sick. If he and Skeeter hadn't argued over the name of the comet, they'd have reported it first. "We missed our chance for glory, Skeeter," he said, "because we were acting like babies."

"Let's never argue like that again," said Skeeter sadly. "Deal?"

"Deal," Doug said.

On the TV, two astronomers were being interviewed.

It was Al and Moo Sleech!

"And what do you two plan to name this new comet?"

"Al and Moo's Comet," said Al.

"Moo and Al's Comet," said Moo.

Al shouted, "No, me first!"

Moo shouted back, "No, me!"

Doug laughed out loud. "Do you believe these guys, Skeeter?"

Skeeter grinned. "Just like babies."